The Lonely Pony

Look for all
the books in the

PET RESCUE CLUB
series

ASPCA kids

PET RESCUE CLUB

The Lonely Pony

by Catherine Hapka

illustrated by Dana Regan

studio fun

A READER'S DIGEST COMPANY

White Plains, New York • Montréal, Québec • Bath, United Kingdom

cover illustration by Steve James
photo courtesy of Geoffrey Tischman

Published by Studio Fun International, Inc.
44 South Broadway, White Plains, NY 10601 U.S.A. and
Studio Fun International Limited,
The Ice House, 124-126 Walcot Street, Bath UK BA1 5BG
Illustration ©2015 Studio Fun International, Inc.
Text ©2015 ASPCA®
Studio Fun Books is a trademark of Studio Fun International, Inc.,
a subsidiary of The Reader's Digest Association, Inc.
Printed in the United States of America.
10 9 8 7 6 5 4 3 2

***The American Society for the Prevention of Cruelty to Animals (ASPCA®)
will receive a minimum guarantee from Studio Fun International, Inc. of $25,000
for the sale of ASPCA® products through December 2017.**

Comments? Questions? Call us at: 1-888-217-3346

Library of Congress Cataloging-in-Publication Data

Hapka, Catherine.

The lonely pony / by Catherine Hapka ; illustrated by Dana Regan.

pages cm. -- (Pet Rescue Club ; 3)

"ASPCA Kids."

Summary: "While out walking a dog one day, Adam notices a shaggy, lonely pony
standing by herself in a field, without food or water. When he continues to see her day
after day, he realizes that this is another case for the Pet Rescue Club--four animal loving
fourth graders who come together to help animals in need in their suburban home
town"-- Provided by publisher.

ISBN 978-0-7944-3452-6 (paperback) -- ISBN 978-0-7944-3454-0 (hard cover)

[1. Ponies--Fiction. 2. Pets--Fiction. 3. Pet adoption--Fiction. 4. Animal shelters--Fiction.
5. Clubs--Fiction.] I. Title.

PZ7.H1996Lon 2015

[Fic]--dc23

2015002875

For Gerri, Ben, Van Gogh, Cassie, and Jack

C.H.

1

At the Shelter

"Oh my gosh, this bunny has to be the cutest animal I've ever seen!" Lolli Simpson exclaimed.

She was in the lobby of the Third Street Animal Shelter with her friends Janey Whitfield and Zach Goldman. The three of them were watching Zach's mother examine a fluffy black-and-white rabbit who was a new shelter resident. Dr. Goldman was a veterinarian with a busy private practice. But she made time each week to donate her skills to the shelter.

Zach looked at Lolli and grinned. "Really?" he said. "Cuter than Roscoe?"

Roscoe was Lolli's dog. He was part Lab, part Rottweiler, and part who-knew-what.

Lolli smiled at Zach. "Okay, the bunny is one of the cutest animals I've ever seen," she said.

But she knew Zach was only teasing her. He loved to joke around and play pranks.

Janey reached out and stroked the rabbit's fur. "He's so soft," she said. "I've never seen a rabbit at the shelter before."

"We do get some in from time to time," said Kitty, the kids' favorite shelter worker. She was a lively young woman with a blonde ponytail. "They can be a little tricky to adopt out."

"Why?" Lolli giggled as the rabbit's little nose twitched. "He's adorable! I already want to take him home myself."

"If Lolli doesn't adopt him, maybe the Pet Rescue Club can help find this bun bun a home," Zach said.

The Pet Rescue Club was a group the three kids had started, along with their friend Adam Santos. The four of them tried to help needy animals in any way they could.

"How did he end up here, anyway?" Lolli asked Kitty. "I can't believe anyone would give up such a sweet pet."

Kitty sighed. "This little guy's previous owners bought him on a whim last Easter," she said. "They thought having a cute little bunny hopping around their house would be fun. But they weren't prepared for how much work a pet like this can be."

"So they took him to the shelter?" Janey said with a frown. "That's vile."

Vile was Janey's new favorite word. She liked to use interesting or unusual words whenever she could.

"How much work could a little bunny like this be?" Lolli wiggled her nose at the rabbit, then smiled as he wiggled his nose in return.

Dr. Goldman glanced up from examining the rabbit's long, floppy ears. "Actually, rabbits require somewhat specialized care," she said. "They need safe housing, and they do best with certain types of foods, and of course every species has its own health and behavior issues."

"Okay, I get it." Lolli tickled the bunny under the chin. "But it would be worth it to have such a cutie pie around the farm! I think I'll ask my parents if I can adopt him."

"Really? That would be fab." Janey looked a little bit wistful, and Lolli knew exactly why. Janey's father was severely allergic to animals, so Janey couldn't have any pets at home. That was how the Pet Rescue Club had come to be. Janey had started a blog asking people to share their cutest pet photos. Someone had posted a picture of a sad, neglected dog named Truman. Janey and her friends had helped Truman find a new home with their homeroom teacher, Ms. Tanaka. The rest was history!

Dr. Goldman gave the bunny one last pat, then stepped back. "He seems healthy," she told Kitty.

"Great. I'll take him back to his cage." Kitty picked up the rabbit, who snuggled into her arms. "Lolli, if you really think you might like to adopt him, we can talk about rabbits' special needs later."

"Okay, thanks," Lolli said. "I need to ask my parents first."

"It'll be cool if you get a pet rabbit,"

Janey said after Kitty had left with the rabbit and Dr. Goldman had gone into the dog room to check on a patient. "I wonder if we could teach him some tricks."

"Yeah, like riding my skateboard!" Zach said with a laugh. "Wait, can rabbits walk on a leash like dogs do? Maybe Adam should expand his business to include walking rabbits, too!"

Adam had a successful pet-sitting and dog-walking business, even though he was only nine. He was a good dog trainer, too. He'd helped Truman learn how to behave better before Ms. Tanaka adopted him.

Janey frowned. "Speaking of Adam, where is he?" She checked her pink watch. "He was supposed to be here ten minutes ago for our meeting."

"I'm sure he'll be here soon," Lolli said. "Saturday is always a busy day for pet sitting. I think he said he had to walk a few dogs after lunch."

"Well, I hope he hurries up and gets here." Janey sounded impatient. "We need to figure out how to find more animals to help, and the weekend's almost half over already!"

Zach pointed at the shelter's front door. "Your wish is our command," he said. "Here comes Adam now."

Adam hurried in. "Sorry I'm late," he said breathlessly. "But I have to tell you guys about—"

"We thought you'd never get here!" Janey interrupted loudly. "I was about to start the meeting without you."

"Okay," Adam said. "But—"

"This is a very important meeting, you know," Janey went on. "Nobody has contacted us since we helped that cat, Hallie, last week. I'm sure there are lots of animals that need our help, but we can't help them if we don't know about them, right? So I was thinking, maybe we should write something on my blog asking people to look for needy animals and e-mail us, or—"

"Janey!" Adam broke in. His voice was

louder than usual. "If you'd let me get two words in, that's what I want to tell you!"

Janey looked surprised at being interrupted. "Huh?"

Adam took a deep breath. "I think I found an animal that needs our help," he said, his voice its normal volume again. "I've noticed her a couple of times while I was out walking dogs. And today I made a special trip to see if she's still there—that's why I was a little late."

"Really?" Lolli said. "What kind of animal is it, Adam? Another dog?"

Adam shook his head. "Definitely not a dog."

"A cat?" Janey said. "Or maybe a rabbit?"

"I bet it's an injured Bigfoot," Zach joked.

Adam just shook his head again. "Come with me and I'll show you," he said.

2

A New Mission

"Are we going to my house?" Lolli joked, peering out the car window.

Dr. Goldman smiled at her in the rearview mirror. "I don't know," she said. "Adam? Should we turn down Lolli's road?"

"No, keep going straight," Adam said. "It's about a mile farther that way."

The Pet Rescue Club had asked Zach's mother to drive them to see Adam's mystery pet. Dr. Goldman had agreed, since she was finished working for the day. She was just as curious to see Adam's mystery animal as everyone else!

Adam had directed them to a rural area right outside of town. Lolli lived nearby on a small farm with her parents, where they grew organic vegetables and kept a sheep and a couple of goats. There were lots of other farms in the area, too. Some grew crops like corn or soybeans. But Janey preferred the ones with cows, horses, or other animals grazing in the fields. There was even a llama farm! Among the farms were some regular houses with extra-large yards.

"Are we there yet?" Janey asked after another few minutes of driving.

"Almost." Adam pointed. "There—turn right onto that road."

Dr. Goldman turned onto a narrow, winding road with no sidewalks or street lamps. There were only a few houses in sight. After a short distance, Adam told her to pull over.

"Is this it?" Janey asked as everyone climbed out of the car.

She looked around. Beside the road was a rickety fence, built half of wood and half of wire. It enclosed a small pen that was choked with weeds. There was a small, tumbledown shed in the middle and a plastic trough half-filled with slimy, greenish water near the gate. On the hillside beyond the pen was a much larger, grassy pasture where a small herd of dairy cows were grazing peacefully.

"Are we here to rescue those cows?" Zach joked. "Because I don't think they'll fit in the dog runs at the shelter."

"Not exactly," Adam said. "The animal

we need to help is right in here."

He waved at the small pen. Janey looked at it again. The only animals she could see in there were some flies buzzing above the water tank.

"Where's the pet who needs rescuing?" Lolli asked. "I don't see anything."

"The animal I saw is probably in that shed." Adam leaned on the fence and whistled loudly.

"I knew it!" Janey said. "It is a dog, isn't it? Adam, I've heard you whistle like that to your clients a million times!"

But Lolli gasped and pointed. "It's not a dog," she cried. "Look!"

An animal had just stepped into view from behind the shed. Janey could hardly believe her eyes. Could that really be…

"Oh my gosh!" she cried. "It's a horse!"

"No way." Zach climbed on the lowest rung of the fence for a better look. "It looks like it shrunk in the wash!"

Lolli smiled. "It's not a horse," she said. "It's a pony!"

Adam looked confused. "You mean a baby horse?"

"Not quite," Dr. Goldman said with a smile.

"A lot of people think a pony is a baby horse. But a pony is actually a horse below a certain height, or sometimes it's a certain breed."

The animal stepped farther out from behind the shed. Whatever you called her, she was the smallest equine Janey had ever

seen! The pony pricked her little ears, then let out a high-pitched whinny and trotted toward them.

"Aw, she's coming to see us!" Janey said. "Here, pony pony!"

"Careful, kids," Dr. Goldman said. "Some ponies bite."

Janey hardly heard her. The pony reached the fence and stuck her muzzle through the wire. When Janey touched the pony's nose, it felt as soft as velvet.

"She's so cute!" Lolli exclaimed.

"Yeah," Adam said. "But look—her mane and tail are all messed up."

Janey saw that he was right. There were brambles tangled in the pony's thick mane and tail. Her hair looked even more snarled than Janey's did after swimming.

"She does look a bit neglected," Dr. Goldman said, peering through the fence at the pony's feet. "Her hooves are long and chipped. And her coat's not in great condition, either."

Janey glanced at the vet. "Wow, you know a lot about ponies! I thought you only treated cats and dogs and other regular pets."

"You're right, I do specialize in small animals." Dr. Goldman shrugged. "But I studied the basics of taking care of large animals in vet school, so I know a little." She reached into her pocket and pulled out a piece of hard candy. "For instance, I learned that most equines love peppermints!"

She unwrapped the candy and held it out, her hand flat with the palm facing up. The pony lipped it up and crunched it.

"You're right, she loves it!" Janey exclaimed. "I think she wants more."

The pony stretched her head over the fence as far as she could. Her ears swiveled back and forth excitedly, and she let out an eager nicker.

Dr. Goldman laughed. "Sorry, girl, that's the only one I have."

Adam smiled, too, but he looked worried. "I've seen this pony in this field every day since I started walking a dog near here last week," he said. "But I've never seen anyone out here feeding her or brushing her or anything."

"Really?" Janey said. "That's totally vile. What if she's been abandoned?"

Lolli gasped. "Abandoned? We have to help her!"

"Let's not jump to conclusions, kids," Dr. Goldman said. "Ponies can get awfully messy in a short time. Maybe she's been rolling in the brambles, and nobody has been by to groom her yet today."

"Come on, Mom," Zach said. "If my hair looked like that, you'd have it tidied up lickety-split." He grinned. "No matter how fast I tried to run away!"

That made everyone laugh, including Dr. Goldman. "I suppose it wouldn't hurt to ask around."

Janey said, "Okay, let's go!"

"Hold on." Dr. Goldman put a hand on Janey's arm. "I'm not sure we should wander around knocking on strangers' doors."

"But we have to do something!" Lolli exclaimed. "We need to help this poor pony!"

"We will," Dr. Goldman said. "I was just going to say, a few of my clients live around here. We could see if any of them are home, and ask if they know who owns her. All right?"

Janey smiled. She should have known Dr. Goldman wouldn't let them down!

"All right!" she exclaimed. "The Pet Rescue Club is on the job! So, let's go!"

3

Lola's Story

The first house they tried was a tidy farmhouse with a big front porch right next to the pony's pen. When Dr. Goldman knocked on the door, the sound of excited yapping came from inside.

"Wow," Adam said. "It sounds like these people have a lot of dogs."

"Five," Dr. Goldman said with a smile. "The Valentines love dogs. They're among my best clients."

A moment later, a plump, pleasant-looking man opened the door. He was in his late sixties, with a bushy gray mustache. Five little dogs danced around his legs.

"Dr. Goldman!" the man exclaimed with a smile. "What a nice surprise! Look, gang, your doctor's here!"

"Oh, your dogs are so cute!" Janey blurted out, bending to pat them as they leaped excitedly around her.

"Hello, Tom," Dr. Goldman said. "Sorry to bother you on a Saturday."

"No bother at all!" He beamed at her. "What can I do for you, doc?"

"We noticed the pony in the pen over there," Dr. Goldman said. "Do you happen to know who owns her?"

The man looked surprised. "As a matter of fact, we do. Her name is Lola."

"Really?" Lolli giggled. "That sounds almost like my name!"

Meanwhile, Janey traded a surprised look with Adam. Mr. Valentine seemed really nice, and his dogs looked happy and healthy. He definitely didn't seem like the type of person who would mistreat a pony on purpose. What was going on?

"This is Lolli, Tom," Dr. Goldman said.

"She's practically your neighbor—her family lives on one of the farms over on Crooked Tree Road." She went on to introduce the other three kids.

"Nice to meet you all," the man said. "I'm Tom Valentine."

"Tom?" a woman's voice called from inside. "Who is at the door?"

A moment later the woman appeared. She was just as plump and pleasant looking as her husband, with wavy hair and bright blue eyes.

"This is my wife, Val," Tom told the kids. "Val, Dr. Goldman and her friends were asking about Lola."

"I didn't realize you two had a pony," Dr. Goldman said. "Have you had her long?"

"Just a few months," Val said. "Why don't you have a seat on the porch and I'll fetch some lemonade. Then we can tell you all about her."

A few minutes later, Dr. Goldman and the Pet Rescue Club members were settled in comfortable wicker furniture with tart, tasty glasses of lemonade. The little dogs were there, too. Two of them were snuggled in Janey's lap. Zach was playing fetch with a third, while the other two took turns running back and forth between Lolli and Adam.

"So," Janey said, scratching one of the dogs behind his silky ears. "Where did you get Lola?"

"She came from the racetrack," Val said.

Zach laughed. "What? That tiny pony

was a racehorse? No way!"

"With those short legs, she must have lost every race," Lolli said with a giggle.

Val laughed, too. "No, Lola wasn't a racehorse, but she lived with one."

"That's right," Tom said. "You see, Lola was a stall companion to a thoroughbred racehorse named Red."

"A stall companion?" Janey wrinkled her nose. "What's that?"

"She was there to keep Red company," Val explained. "All the sights and sounds of the track made him nervous, but having Lola in the stall with him kept him much calmer and happier."

Dr. Goldman nodded. "I know what you mean. Part of my clinical work in vet school took me to the racetrack. On one of my visits there I vaccinated and dewormed a goat who was the companion to a pretty successful racehorse."

"Wow," Janey said. She'd never heard of such a thing! "So why isn't Lola still at the racetrack helping Red?"

"Because Red retired from racing a few months ago," Val said, taking a sip of her lemonade. "His owners gave him to a young local woman who retrains racehorses for new careers as riding horses."

"I've heard about that," Lolli said. "My parents donated some hay to a group that helps racehorses find new homes after they're retired."

"Yes, well, this young woman does marvelous work," Tom said. "At least that's what Red's old racing trainer tells me. Unfortunately, Red's new trainer wasn't able to take Lola. And his old race trainer had no use for Lola once Red was gone, since none of his other horses needed a companion."

"Poor Lola," Adam said.

"Yeah," Zach said. "She got laid off from her job, and had nowhere to go."

"Exactly." Tom poured everyone a little

more lemonade. "The race trainer is an old fishing buddy of mine, and he knows that Val and I are animal lovers." He smiled and bent to pat one of the little dogs. "Obviously!"

"Tom had also mentioned to him how I loved reading horse books as a child," Val put in. "So he asked if we'd be interested in having Lola." She sighed. "The trouble is, he didn't tell us just how much time, money, and hard work it takes to keep a horse—even a small one!"

Tom nodded. "We just can't keep up with it all," he said. "Not with my bad knees and Val's busy volunteering schedule. We've been meaning to ask around for help, but haven't quite found the time."

Janey bit her lip and glanced at her

friends. It sounded as if Tom and Val had meant to do a nice thing by taking Lola in. But they'd gotten in over their heads.

"I see," Dr. Goldman said with a sympathetic smile. "Did you ask the trainer to take her back?"

"He can't," Tom said. "He suggested we ask around town to see if anyone wants poor old Lola."

"You don't have to do that," Janey blurted out. " We can do that for you! The Pet Rescue Club will help you find Lola the perfect new home!"

4

Project Pony

Val looked surprised. "The what club?" she said. "Oh, but never mind—I don't want to bother you kids with our problems."

Her husband smiled at Janey and the others. "Yes, we'll work it out."

"No, really!" Zach said. "We have a club that helps pets find new homes and stuff."

"They really do," Dr. Goldman said with a nod. "They've helped several local pets already." She told the couple about Truman and the other animals the Pet Rescue Club had helped.

Val looked impressed. "How wonderful! What do you think, Tom? Maybe they can help us after all."

"We definitely can," Janey said. "Lola is so cute, I'm sure it won't take long at all to find her the perfect new home."

"What a relief," Val exclaimed. "See, we're scheduled to leave on a road trip in about a week to visit our son. He lives out of state, so we were planning to stay for a couple of weeks."

"That's right," Tom added. "We were worried we'd have to hurry to find something to do with Lola before we leave."

"Well, now you don't have to worry," Janey said. "Not with the Pet Rescue Club on the job." She knew they would have to work fast to find Lola a new home before the Valentines left on their trip next week. But she was sure they could do it.

"Terrific," Tom said. "Can you take her today?"

"Today?" Janey gulped and glanced at the others. "Um…"

"We could call the shelter and see if they can take Lola in," Lolli suggested.

"Yeah." Zach grinned. "She's not any bigger than a Great Dane or something. She'd totally fit in one of the large dog runs!"

"Well, I've never seen a horse there, but I suppose it wouldn't hurt to ask." Dr. Goldman dug into her pocket. "Here, you can use my cell phone."

Janey took the phone and dialed the familiar number. When Kitty answered, she explained the situation.

"We were hoping you could keep Lola at the shelter until we find her a home," Janey finished. "It probably won't take long."

"I'm sorry, Janey," Kitty said. "I'm afraid we don't have the facilities to take care of farm animals—not even small ones. I could call the shelter over in Lakeville for you, though. They have a couple of goats and a potbellied pig there right now, and I'm pretty sure they've taken in horses in the past."

"Lakeville?" Janey clutched the phone to her ear. "But that's almost an hour's drive away! How can we help her if she's not even close by?"

"What?" Zach whispered loudly, poking her on the arm. "What's she saying? What was that about Lakeville?"

"Ssh!" Janey hushed him. Kitty was talking again. "I'm sorry, could you repeat that? Zach was yapping in my ear."

Kitty chuckled. "I said, I could ask around about finding a foster home—maybe one of the farms outside of town could keep her for a few days."

"That sounds good. Hang on, let me tell the others." Janey lowered the phone. "Kitty says maybe she can help us find a foster home for Lola. She thinks one of the farms around here might be willing to take her in until we find her a permanent home."

"That's a good idea," Dr. Goldman said, and the Valentines nodded.

But Lolli gasped. "Wait," she exclaimed. "I live on a farm!"

Janey blinked at her. "Um, yeah, we

know." Then she gasped, too. "Wait! Are you saying—"

"What if I'm the foster home?" Lolli cried before Janey could finish. "Me and my parents, I mean. We have plenty of room in our pasture. And we already have the goats and sheep, so a tiny little horse wouldn't even be that much extra trouble."

"Perfect! I'll tell Kitty," Janey said.

"Wait," Dr. Goldman stopped her. Then she turned to Lolli. "I think we need to ask your parents about this. Do they have any experience taking care of horses?"

"I don't think so," Lolli said. "But they've had lots of other animals."

Zach's mom still looked dubious. "I know. But horses are a lot of work—more than most animals. You have to be careful about what you feed them, and they need their feet trimmed back every couple of months or so...."

"Yes, that's right," Val put in. "We never did get around to finding anyone to do the foot trimming."

Tom nodded. "Been meaning to call the race trainer to ask for his help, but he's awfully hard to reach."

"We won't have Lola long enough to worry about that sort of stuff," Janey told Dr. Goldman. "It'll just be for a few days."

Dr. Goldman scratched her chin. "Well, I suppose it's up to your parents," she told Lolli. "You'd better call them and see if they want to take this on."

"Kitty? We might know about a foster farm," Janey said into the phone. "We'll call you back in a minute, okay?" She hung up and handed the phone to Lolli. "Call your parents right now. I'm sure they'll say yes!" She crossed her fingers as her friend took the phone.

Soon Lolli was talking to her father. She told him about Lola and what Kitty had said about finding a foster home. "She wouldn't be any trouble at all," she finished. "The Pet Rescue Club would do all the work to take care of her. It will probably only be for a day or two."

Janey couldn't hear what Mr. Simpson said. But when Lolli hung up, she was smiling. "Dad said it's okay as long as we do all the work."

"Oh, thank you!" Val exclaimed. "I can't tell you what a load off our minds this is, kids."

Janey grinned at her. "You're welcome. I'll call Kitty and tell her."

When Janey hung up a moment later, Dr. Goldman stood up. "Thanks for the lemonade, Tom and Val," she said. "We'd better get going if we want to get Lola settled in tonight."

"Yeah, let's go tell her the good news!" Zach exclaimed. He raced off down the porch steps. The little dogs all barked and raced after him.

"Come back, you rascals!" Tom whistled loudly, and the dogs turned around and ran back to him.

Adam patted a couple of them. "They're well trained," he said admiringly.

"And cute." Janey grabbed the smallest dog for one last snuggle. "Thanks for the lemonade, Mr. and Mrs. Valentine. We'd better go get Lola!"

"We'll come along and say good-bye," Val said. "Just let us put the dogs in the house first."

Janey waited impatiently while the couple herded the excited dogs back inside. Then the whole group hurried back down the road.

When they arrived at the pen, Lola was

still standing by the fence. "Look, she was waiting for us," Lolli said.

"She must have known we were coming back to get her," Zach said. "Come on, it's time to go to your new foster farm!"

Adam blinked. "Yeah, but wait," he said. "How are we going to get her there?"

5

Travel Plans

Janey didn't know why her friends looked so worried. "It's not very far to Lolli's farm," she said. "And Lola is little. Why can't we just put her in the back of the car? That's how we'd carry a dog the same size, right?"

Dr. Goldman glanced at her hatchback, which was still parked beside the road. "Uh, I don't think so," she said. "Lola may be small, but she's not a dog. Her hooves will make a mess of my upholstery."

"Yeah" Zach grinned. "Besides, horses aren't house-trained."

"Don't you mean car-trained?" Lolli joked.

Janey looked at Val and Tom. "How do you take her places?" she asked.

"We don't." Tom shrugged. "My race-track friend dropped her off here with a big horse trailer."

"Oh." Janey bit her lip. "Well, maybe we can find someone with a pickup truck we could borrow. Lola could jump into the back and ride over that way."

Adam looked alarmed. "That doesn't sound very safe for Lola," he said. "What if she jumps out while we're driving?"

"We could ride back there with her and hold her in," Zach suggested.

"No," Dr. Goldman said immediately. "Out of the question. That would be much too dangerous."

Tom sighed. "Sorry, kids. Maybe we need to leave Lola to the experts after all. The shelter in Lakeville might have a trailer they can use to pick her up."

"No!" Lolli's eyes filled with tears. "I

really want her to come to my house."

"I understand, dear," Val said kindly. "But if we can't get her there…"

Janey frowned. Why did this have to be so complicated? All they needed to do was transport Lola a mile or so down the road….

"I've got it!" she blurted out. "We can do it the old-fashioned way."

"You mean hitch Lola up to a wagon and drive her back that way?" Zach said. "Cool!"

Janey shook her head. "We don't need a wagon," she said. "We can just walk her to Lolli's place."

"I suppose we could, at that," Dr. Goldman said. "It's not very far. Probably less than a mile."

Tom looked relieved. "I think we have a halter and lead rope around here somewhere. Let me take a look."

He let himself into the pen. Lola followed him halfway to the shed, but when Zach called her name the pony returned to the kids.

Janey patted Lola as Tom disappeared into the shed. A minute later he emerged holding a tangle of dingy straps.

"Found it!" he called, hurrying back. "Now, if I can just remember how to put this thing on…"

"I think I can help." Dr. Goldman smiled and let herself into the pen. "At least I learned that much about horses in vet school!"

It only took her and Tom a moment to figure out how to put on and latch the pony's halter. Then Tom clipped the lead rope to the metal ring beneath Lola's chin.

"There you are, Lola." He gave the pony a pat. "Ready to go to your new foster home?"

Adam held the gate open as Lola followed Tom toward it. As soon as she went through, she yanked her head down and started nibbling on the long grass at the edge of the road.

"Looks like she's hungry," Lolli said.

Tom gave a tug on the lead rope. "Come on, Lola. You can eat when you get to Lolli's place."

The pony ignored him and kept eating. "Here, let me try," Zach said, grabbing the rope. He tried to pull Lola's head up, but it stayed where it was. "Wow, she's stronger than she looks!"

"Come on, Lola," Janey cooed, leaning

closer. "Don't you want to come with us?"

"Yeah, you'll love Lolli's place," Adam added. "Come on, girl!" He let out a whistle.

That got Lola's attention. She lifted her head to look at Adam. At the same time, Zach gave another tug on the rope. The pony took a step forward.

"It's working!" Janey cried. "Keep going!"

Zach walked a few steps. Lola followed him.

"Good luck, kids," Tom called. "We'll stop over in a little while with her leftover hay and things."

"Great," Dr. Goldman said. "Maybe you can give me a ride back to my car then."

She started giving the Valentines directions to Lolli's house. Janey kept moving, staying beside Lola and urging her to keep walking.

For a while, Lola seemed willing to let the kids lead her along beside the road. But then she spotted a tasty patch of clover and lowered her head again.

"Lola, no!" Lolli cried. "We'll never get there if you stop to eat every few steps."

Dr. Goldman caught up and helped the kids get Lola moving again. But once again, the pony stopped after a minute or two to eat more grass.

"How does anyone ever get a horse anywhere?" Janey exclaimed.

"Most horses must not be as hungry as Lola," Lolli guessed.

Zach grinned. "Now I know why there's no grass growing on racetracks," he said. "All the horses would just run out of the starting gate and start eating!"

"Actually, I saw a racetrack on TV once that was grass," Adam said.

Janey frowned at them. "Would you stop talking about racetracks and help keep Lola moving? Otherwise this will take all night!"

"Sorry," Adam said. "Lola—heel! Heel, girl!" He patted his leg, like he did to signal a dog to follow him.

But Lola ignored him. "She's not a dog, Adam," Janey said. "She probably doesn't know what 'heel' means."

"Is there another word they use to get horses to heel?" Lolli wondered. "Gallop, Lola! Trot!"

The pony didn't respond except to move a step forward to a nicer patch of grass. Janey sighed and wiped her forehead. It was a warm afternoon, and she was starting to sweat.

"We haven't gone very far," Dr. Goldman said. "Do you want to turn back and tell the Valentines this isn't going to work?"

That made Janey forget all about how hot she was. "No!" she said. "We'll get her there." Glancing at Lola, she muttered, "Eventually."

6

Special Needs

Eventually, they made it. It took a long time, but finally the Pet Rescue Club reached Lolli's long gravel driveway. The kids had taken turns leading Lola, and it was Janey's turn right then. She kept the pony in the middle of the drive so she wouldn't be tempted to try to eat the grass growing alongside it. Lola looked from side to side as she walked. Janey guessed that the pony was checking out the orchard of fruit trees on one side of her and the big fenced-in pasture on the other side.

Lolli's parents were waiting halfway up the driveway, with Roscoe sitting beside them. The family's sheep and two goats were right on the other side of the fence nearby, staring curiously at the new arrivals.

When Roscoe spotted the pony, he jumped up and barked. His tail wagged, and he tried to run forward. But Lolli's father had

him on a leash, and held him back.

"We were just getting worried," Lolli's mother called. "Oh, that pony is adorable!"

"I know, right?" Lolli said. "She doesn't like walking on a leash, though."

"Yeah," Zach said. "She definitely needs a few training sessions with Adam."

"Never mind that." Now that they had arrived, Janey couldn't wait to get into a nice, air-conditioned house and have a snack. "Let's put her in the pasture and then go take a rest."

"Not so fast," Dr. Goldman said. "You can't just toss her in a pasture."

"Why not?" Zach said. "Isn't that where horses live?"

"Yes, but Lola has been in that small, weedy pen for a few months now," Dr. Goldman reminded the kids. "She's not used to eating lots of nice, rich grass. In vet school, we learned that horses' stomachs are surprisingly delicate. Eating too much really nice grass right now could make Lola very sick."

Janey was surprised. She'd never heard about anything like that. But she trusted Dr. Goldman.

"Besides, there could also be some weeds out there that she shouldn't eat," Lolli's mother said.

Adam glanced at the sheep and goats. "But those guys eat out there all the time."

"Yes, but sheep and goats have very different digestive systems from ponies," Dr. Goldman said. "They can eat a lot of weeds and plants that would poison Lola."

Janey's heart sank. "So what can we do to keep Lola safe?" she asked. "I don't want her to eat something poisonous!"

"We have some extra fencing stuff in the barn," Lolli's father spoke up. "You kids could build her a little pen inside the pasture."

"That's a great idea." Dr. Goldman smiled at him. "If you build it in a spot where the grass is a little sparser, Lola can graze safely without being able to eat too much rich stuff. And you can make it small enough to check for any possibly dangerous weeds and remove any you find."

"And feed them to the goats," Zach added, scratching one of the goats over the fence.

Janey sighed, glancing at the house. Her stomach rumbled.

But Janey wanted to help Lola, and that meant her empty stomach would have to wait. "Okay," she said, squaring her shoulders. "Let's build a pen."

Lolli's father helped the kids fetch some step-in fence posts and a couple of rolls of woven wire. "This stuff might not hold a full-sized horse," he said, scratching his head uncertainly. "But it should be good enough for a pony like Lola."

Lolli's mother put Roscoe in the house. Then she returned and held Lola's lead rope, letting the pony nibble on the short grass beside the driveway while her husband, Dr. Goldman, and the kids got to work on the fence. Before long Janey was sweating more than ever. Building fences was hard work!

But every time she wanted to quit, she

just looked over at Lola. That made her work even harder.

It took a long time, but finally the pen was ready. They'd built it along one side of the barn, where there was a deep overhang that Lola could use for shelter if the sun got too strong.

"Perfect!" Lolli's father declared at last. "Want to check it out, Lola?"

Dr. Goldman led the pony into the pen. She took off the lead rope and left Lola to explore.

Lola sniffed at the gate as Lolli shut it. Then she turned and looked around the pen. The goats and sheep were standing in their pasture on the other side of Lola's new fence, looking in. Lola whinnied at them, then trotted over to say hello through the wire. After that, she started to graze on her side of the fence, while the other animals nibbled the grass on their side.

Dr. Goldman smiled. "Ponies and horses are herd animals. Lola is probably happy to have company after being by herself for a couple of months."

"Maybe we can find her a home with other ponies," Adam said.

"Yeah." Janey glanced at Lolli's house. "Since Lola is having a snack, maybe it's time for us to have one, too?"

"Soon," Lolli's mother said. "You still need to set up a tub with water. And there's not much grass in the pen—won't we need hay?"

"The Valentines are bringing the supplies they have." Dr. Goldman shaded her hand against the late afternoon sun and peered down the driveway. "A-ha! Here they are, right on cue!"

A moment later, an SUV pulled to a stop nearby. Tom hopped out of the driver's seat. "Oh, look at that!" he exclaimed as he saw Lola. "She's found some friends."

The back of the SUV was crammed with hay bales, and there was a big, black tub for water in the backseat. "Come on, kids," Dr. Goldman said. "Let's get this stuff unloaded."

Half an hour later, Janey was so exhausted she wanted to lie down on the grass and take a nap. She and her friends had hauled the heavy bales of hay into the barn. They'd dragged the water tub into the pen, then hooked up the hose to fill it. They'd opened one of the hay bales and carried part of it out for Lola to eat. They'd found a spare shelf in the barn to store the grooming tools, a spare halter, and a few other items Tom had brought.

Meanwhile, Dr. Goldman had left with Tom, promising to return with her car to drive them all home. Janey couldn't wait!

But when she looked at Lola and saw her nibbling hay or grass, or sipping water, Janey felt happy and satisfied. "Lola is so cute," she told Lolli as they watched the pony. "I'm sure it won't take long to find her the perfect new home."

Lolli nodded, looking just as tired as Janey felt. "I'm glad she's here, even if she's a lot of work."

Janey giggled. "After this, taking care of Roscoe will seem super easy! Oh, and your new bunny, too, if you get him."

"Yeah." Lolli shot a look at her parents, who were helping the boys put away the hose. "Still, I think I'll wait and ask if I can get the bunny until after Lola goes to her new home."

7

Barn Chores

"Here we are, Farmer Janey," Janey's father joked as he pulled into Lolli's driveway the next day. "Better get going on your chores!"

Janey smiled. "Thanks for the ride, Daddy."

She jumped out of the car. Adam and Zach were already there with Lolli, watching Lola eat grass in her pen. They'd come straight over after Adam's morning dog-walking jobs.

"You're late," Zach called when he spotted Janey. "But don't worry, we saved all the stinky pony manure for you."

"Gee, thanks." Janey rolled her eyes.

"How's Lola?"

"Great," Lolli said. "After we feed her and clean up her pen, maybe we can use those brushes Mr. Valentine sent to groom her."

Janey nodded. "Good idea. We want her to look good for her photo session."

"What photo session?" Adam asked.

Janey held up her tablet. "I want to take some pictures of her to put on the blog. That will help her find a home faster."

"Good idea." Lolli picked up a pitchfork. "But first, let's get to work."

The kids worked hard. They cleaned up all the manure Lola had made overnight, using the pitchfork to put it in a wheelbarrow and then dumping it in the compost pile behind the barn. They scrubbed out the water tub and filled it again. They put out more hay.

"Okay." Lolli brushed hay off her hands. "Now for the fun part!"

She hurried into the barn and fetched the bucket of grooming tools. There were several brushes, a wide-toothed comb, a hoof pick, and a bottle of spray-on conditioner.

"Get ready for your beauty treatment, Lola!" Janey sang out as the kids entered the pen.

Lola was eating the pile of hay the kids had set out. She barely looked up when they started brushing her.

"Good girl," Janey said. "You want to look pretty, don't you?"

Adam leaned over to peer at the pony's

tangled mane. "I think I'll try getting some of these burrs out."

"Good idea," Janey said. "Her mane looks totally vile."

She handed Adam the comb. He grabbed it and got to work.

After close to an hour, the pony looked much better. Janey stepped back to survey their work.

"She looks great," she said. "See if you can get her to keep her head up so I can get some good pictures."

They spent the next several minutes on the photo shoot. It wasn't easy, since the pony preferred eating over posing. But finally Janey got some cute photos of Lola.

"Want me to upload them for you?" Zach offered.

Janey nodded and handed over the tablet. Zach knew just about everything about computers and technology, so she knew he'd do a good job of cropping and positioning the photos.

"Thanks," she said. "You can upload the

text I wrote, too, okay?" She pointed out the file on the desktop.

"Sure," Zach said as he got to work.

Lolli peered over his shoulder. "What'd you write?" she asked.

"Just a short entry about Lola," Janey said. "I did it last night after dinner. Zach can read it to you when it posts."

A second later, Zach cleared his throat and started to read: "'Meet Lola, the cutest little pony on the planet! And guess what? She's looking for a new home, so some lucky person will get to pet her adorable face every day! Contact the Pet Rescue Club if you want to be that person! Lola can't wait to meet her new best friend!'"

"How does that sound?" Janey asked the others.

"Fine, I guess," Adam said. "I've never had to write an ad for a pony before."

"Yeah." Lolli looked over Zach's shoulder as the first photo appeared below the text. "Anyway, it hardly matters what we write. As soon as people see those pictures, they'll be lining up to take Lola home!"

"Rise and shine, pony girl!"

Lolli cracked one eye open and saw her mother opening her window shades. "What time is it?" she mumbled.

"Time to go out and take care of the pony," her mother replied cheerfully. "You'll have to hurry to get everything done before it's time to leave for school."

"Okay." Lolli yawned and sat up. It felt as if she'd barely slept at all! But she knew Lola needed her, so she dragged herself out of bed and pulled on her clothes.

Lolli woke up a little when Lola spotted her coming and let out her cute high-pitched nicker. The goats and sheep trotted over to say hello, too. Being out with the animals so early in the morning made Lolli feel like a real farmer!

"Good morning, Lola," she said with a smile. "Ready for your breakfast?"

She pulled more hay off the bale and carried it out to the pen. While Lola was eating, Lolli picked up the pony's manure as fast as she could. Luckily there was still plenty of water in the tub, so Lolli figured her friends could help her dump out the leftover water and then scrub and refill the tub after school. By the time she finished everything her arms were tired from picking up manure and scratchy from the hay, and she was pretty sure she didn't smell her best. But there was no time for a shower if she wanted to be on time for school.

"Got to go, Lola," she said, blowing the pony a kiss. "See you this afternoon!"

By the time she arrived at school, Lolli was already yawning. But she felt more alert when Janey rushed over with big news.

"We're getting tons of hits on the blog post about Lola!" Janey reported, holding up her tablet. "See? It's just like I predicted—tons of people want to adopt Lola already!"

"Really?" Lolli smiled, knowing all her hard work that morning had been worth it. "Hooray!"

8

Help from Ms. Tanaka

"Did any more messages come in about Lola?" Lolli asked Janey after school.

The two girls and Zach were waiting for Lolli's father to pick them up. They were going to Lolli's farm to do the afternoon pony chores. Adam was meeting them there after he finished taking care of his afternoon dog-sitting clients.

"Yes—three more since I checked this morning," Janey reported. "Let's read them and see which person sounds the best."

She brought up the first message and scanned it. Lolli was reading over her shoulder.

"Wow," Lolli commented. "I'm not sure this one is serious."

"Yeah," Zach said. "The girl thinks she can keep Lola in her bedroom like a dog or a cat." He laughed. "She must not know how much a little pony can poop!"

"Ew!" Janey made a face at him. "Never mind—here's another one."

She scanned the next message:

I always wanted a pony like Lola! But I need to change her name to Rebel. That's because I'm going to take her to the rodeo and use her to rope cows like a real cowboy. Please write back and tell me when you can bring her to my house. Thanks, Robert.

"Roping cows at the rodeo?" Lolli said. "I don't think Lola would be very good at that!"

"Yeah," Zach said. "Roscoe would be a better rodeo horse than Lola." He laughed. "My cat Mulberry would probably even be better!"

Lolli took the tablet from Janey and scrolled back to the earlier messages, reading over them quickly. "Some of the people who wrote earlier sound okay, at least," she said. "This girl says she has a really big backyard with lots of grass. And this other one says she's ridden ponies at the fair a bunch of times so she knows all about them."

"Okay," Zach said. "So how do we decide who gets her?"

"We'll figure it out," Janey said. "But let's wait a little longer so more people have a chance to see her."

....

All day Tuesday, Lolli couldn't stop yawning. She and the rest of the Pet Rescue Club went to her farm right after school to take care of Lola. Lolli started pulling some hay off a bale, but she had to stop and yawn three

times in a row.

"Are we keeping you awake?" Zach joked. "Maybe you should take a nap on that hay instead of feeding it to Lola."

"Sorry." Lolli stifled another yawn. "I'm not used to getting up so early every day to do chores."

Adam nodded. "I know what you mean. When I first started dog-walking before school, it was hard to wake up sometimes."

"Never mind," Janey put in. "We got a bunch more messages about Lola today. Some of them sound pretty good."

Zach grinned. "No more rodeo riders?"

"No more rodeo riders." Janey rolled her eyes. "I wrote back to that kid Robert and told him Lola didn't want to be a rodeo pony."

"So how are we going to figure out who

gets to take Lola home?" Lolli asked.

Janey bit her lip. "I'm not sure," she said. "Maybe we should ask Ms. Tanaka for help."

"Our homeroom teacher?" Adam looked surprised. "Why?"

"She told us she used to ride horses when she was younger, remember?" Lolli said. "Asking her is a great idea, Janey!"

She only wished Ms. Tanaka was there to ask right away. Maybe that way Lola could find a home today and Lolli wouldn't have to wake up early again tomorrow!

But when she looked at Lola nibbling her hay, Lolli decided she really didn't mind one more early morning. Not if it meant finding the perfect home for the sweet little pony.

By the time school ended on Wednesday, several more messages had come in about Lola. "Good," Janey told Lolli as the two girls walked outside together. "That way Ms. Tanaka will have plenty to look at. Look, there she is!"

Ms. Tanaka was one of the bus monitors that day. Janey and Lolli waited until she'd finished helping some first graders get on their bus. Then they hurried over and told her what was going on.

"You took in a pony?" Ms. Tanaka looked impressed. "Wow, I didn't realize you kids knew how to take care of horses!"

"We don't," Lolli admitted.

"At least we didn't," Janey added. "We're learning fast."

"Yeah. But we need help figuring out who should get her," Lolli said. "Can you help us? We were hoping you could read the messages and help us figure out who sounds the best."

"Sure, I'll take a look. Just give me a minute to finish up here, okay?" Ms. Tanaka said.

Ten minutes later all the buses were gone and Ms. Tanaka was scanning the messages on Janey's tablet. The more she read, the more worried she looked.

"Oh, dear," she said at last. "To be honest, kids, I'm not sure any of these sound like a good home for a horse—not even a tiny one."

"Really?" Janey's heart sank. "Are you sure?"

"Sorry." Ms. Tanaka scanned the messages again. "Most of these people sound nice and well-meaning, but none of them mention having any experience with horses."

"What about the girl who says she's ridden lots of ponies?" Janey said.

Ms. Tanaka shook her head. "Going on pony rides at the fair isn't the same as taking care of a pony full time," she explained.

"Lola needs a knowledgeable caretaker to keep her healthy and happy."

"But we didn't know anything about taking care of ponies," Janey argued. "And look how great Lola is doing with us!"

"It's only been a couple of days, right?" Ms. Tanaka said gently. "That's not the same as committing to a pony's lifetime."

"Oh." Lolli bit her lip. "So how do we find someone knowledgeable about ponies?"

The teacher scrolled back and read Janey's blog entry. "Well, you might need to adjust your ad a little," she said. "Focus less on how cute Lola is, and more on her needs in a home."

"Okay." Janey sighed. "Could you help me do that?"

Ms. Tanaka smiled. "Sure. But in exchange, you have to let me meet Lola. Okay?"

Janey smiled. "It's a deal!"

....

"Truman!" Janey cried as a cute little dog jumped out of Ms. Tanaka's car.

The Pet Rescue Club was at the farm again. While waiting for Ms. Tanaka, they'd done the afternoon chores. Lola was eating her hay while Lolli brushed her. Lolli's father was there, too, fixing a piece of the fence that had come loose.

Truman raced over to greet the kids, barking and wagging his tail. Janey hugged him. "I'm glad you brought Truman along," she told Ms. Tanaka, giggling as Truman licked her chin.

Ms. Tanaka smiled. "Truman loves going places," she said. She greeted Mr. Simpson and the other kids. Then she stepped toward the pen. "Oh, you were right—Lola is adorable!"

The pony took one more bite of hay, then wandered over to say hello. Ms. Tanaka scratched Lola's neck, which made her stretch out and grunt happily.

"Hey, she likes that!" Zach exclaimed.

"Horses usually love having their itchy spots scratched," Ms. Tanaka said with a chuckle. She glanced at the pony's hooves. "Oh, dear, it looks as if Lola hasn't had her feet done in quite a while."

"Yeah, Zach's mom said something about that, too," Adam said. "Can you show us how to do it?"

Ms. Tanaka shook her head. "That's a job for an expert," she said. "Lola will need to see a farrier soon—that's another name for a horseshoer, or a blacksmith. She's probably also behind on her shots and deworming, and might even need her teeth floated."

"Floated?" Zach laughed. "Lola's pretty small for a horse, but she's too big to fit in the bathtub!"

Ms. Tanaka laughed, too. "Floating is the term for a horse getting her teeth filed down," she explained. "If it isn't done regularly, her teeth can get sharp and cut her mouth when she tries to eat."

"Oh." Janey bit her lip. "I guess that's not something we can do ourselves, either?"

"No, sorry." The teacher shrugged. "You'll need either a vet or a special horse dentist."

Lolli's father had been listening. "All this is starting to sound expensive," he commented.

"Yes. Keeping a pony isn't cheap." Ms. Tanaka looked sympathetic. She rubbed the pony's shaggy mane and glanced at the kids. "If Lola stays with the Pet Rescue Club much longer, you'll probably need to think about how to raise enough money to pay for her care."

"Yeah." Janey traded an anxious look with her friends.

What had they gotten themselves into?

9

Horsing Around

Lolli could tell that her father was worried about what Ms. Tanaka had said. "It's okay," she said quickly. "We can have a fundraiser. Right, guys?"

"Yeah!" Zach and Janey said at the same time, while Adam nodded.

But Lolli's dad shook his head. "I don't know, kids," he said. "This might be more than we can handle. Lola really needs to be with knowledgeable horse people. We should probably call the shelter in Lakeville —it sounds like they have people there who know how to take care of horses."

"No!" Lolli cried. "We want to help Lola ourselves!"

"Yeah, tons of people have already seen her on the blog," Janey said.

Lolli's dad looked dubious. "But you told me you haven't heard from anyone who sounded right for Lola."

"Ms. T is going to help us write a better ad," Zach told him. "Right, Ms. T?"

Ms. Tanaka was staring thoughtfully at Lola. "I might be able to do better than that," she said. "I just had an idea."

Lolli's heart jumped. "What is it?"

"I just remembered—an old friend of mine keeps her horses at a stable not far from here," the teacher said. "I could call her and see if she'd be willing to help find a new home for Lola."

"Really?" Adam said. "That would be great!"

Janey held her breath while Ms. Tanaka pulled out her cell phone. Just then the goats started head-butting each other and making a lot of noise. Ms. Tanaka stepped away behind the barn where Janey couldn't hear what she was saying.

"Do you think her friend can help?" Lolli wondered, watching as her father waved his hands to shoo the goats away.

"I hope so." Janey gazed at Lola, who was nibbling at some grass beneath the fence. "Because it would be totally vile if Lola had to go to the shelter in Lakeville."

"Yeah," Zach agreed. "Especially after all the work we've been doing!"

A moment later Ms. Tanaka returned. She was smiling. "Good news," she told the kids. "Darby is at the stable right now. She's showing a horse to a potential buyer. But she said we could come on over and she'll talk to us about Lola after she's done."

"What are we waiting for?" Zach exclaimed. "Let's go!"

Ms. Tanaka left Truman at Lolli's house so he could play with Roscoe while they were gone. Then Mr. Simpson drove everyone over in his big old station wagon. On the way, Ms. Tanaka explained that she and Darby had grown up riding together.

"I haven't seen her in a few years, since we're both so busy," she said. "But I heard she's training horses professionally now."

"Just like Adam!" Zach said with a grin. "Only horses instead of dogs."

Mr. Simpson chuckled. "I think we're here."

Janey looked out the window. They were passing a sign for the boarding stable. The driveway curved around some trees and ended by a large riding ring with a pretty green barn beyond. A woman was riding a tall, handsome chestnut horse in the ring.

"Is that her?" Janey asked, squinting at the rider. It was hard to see the woman's face clearly beneath her riding helmet, but she looked at least ten years older than Ms. Tanaka.

"No, Darby's over there, standing by the gate," Ms. Tanaka said, pointing to a woman around her age wearing a baseball cap, tall boots, and sunglasses. "The woman on the horse must be her client."

As soon as they all got out of the car, the younger woman spotted them and waved. "Hi!" she cried, hurrying over to meet them as they reached the ring fence. She gave Ms. Tanaka a big hug. "It's so good to see you! I'm glad you came. We'll be finished here soon."

Ms. Tanaka hugged her back, then introduced everyone. "Don't worry, we'll stay out of your way until you're done," she added.

"No worries," Darby said. "Mrs. Jamison is just trying out this fellow one more time before taking him home."

"What a beautiful horse!" Lolli exclaimed. "Why in the world are you selling him?"

"Lolli!" her father chided. "That's not polite."

Darby laughed. "It's okay," she said. "I'm

selling him because I love helping ex-race-horses find new careers and new people to love them."

"That's a racehorse?" Adam sounded surprised.

Janey was surprised, too. The horse was trotting slowly in a circle, his neck arched proudly. He looked nothing like the lean, fast horses she'd seen racing on TV.

"He used to be a racehorse." Darby smiled as she watched the horse slow to a walk. "Now Red is turning into a wonderful riding horse."

"Red?" Janey could hardly believe her ears. "Did you say that horse's name is Red?"

Zach looked excited. "And he used to be a racehorse?"

Lolli gasped. "I think we know your

horse's best friend!"

Janey, Lolli, Zach, and Adam all started talking at once. Darby looked confused for a second. But when Ms. Tanaka started to explain about Lola, her eyes widened.

"Hang on," she said. "Are you talking about the cute little Shetland pony companion I saw with Red at the track?"

"Yes, that's Lola!" Janey said. "Red's old trainer gave her to some people who couldn't keep her. So now we're trying to find her a home."

Lolli's father nodded. "The trouble is, we're not really equipped to take care of a pony."

"Oh, dear." Darby looked sad. "I wish I could have taken Lola. But I'm not allowed to keep two horses in one stall here, even if one of them is tiny. And the stable is full right now—no extra stalls."

Zach glanced at Red, who was walking past the spot where they were standing. "Do you think Red misses Lola? We heard they were best friends."

Red's rider brought him to a stop. "Hello," she said with a smile. "I couldn't help overhearing some of your conversation...."

"Sorry," Zach said. "I get that a lot. My mom says I'm louder than a howler monkey with a megaphone."

The woman chuckled. "No, it's fine," she said. "But what was that you were saying about Red's best friend?"

Darby repeated what the kids had just

told her. "It seems Lola has lost her home, and these nice kids are trying to find her another one," she said. "I'm hoping I can help."

The woman patted Red. "So this fellow had a pony as a friend? How charming!" She smiled at Janey and the others. "Is there any way I could meet this Lola?"

10

Together Again

"Of course you can meet Lola!" Janey blurted out.

"She's at Lolli's house," Zach added. "It's only a couple of miles from here."

Lolli nodded. "Maybe you can help us look for a new owner, too!"

"Maybe I can." Mrs. Jamison winked at Darby. "There might not be any extra stalls here, but I happen to have a couple open in my barn at home."

"You have a barn at your house?" Janey

asked, feeling a twinge of excitement. "Does that mean you're an experienced horse person?"

Mrs. Jamison laughed. "I like to think I know what I'm doing, at least a little bit."

"Mrs. Jamison is being modest," Darby said with a smile. "She's owned horses all her life—she's as experienced as they come."

"I don't know about that," Mrs. Jamison said. "But I do know I have a couple of young children who might love a tiny equine of their very own."

Janey could hardly believe her ears. Had they just found the perfect new owner for Lola?

"What are we waiting for?" she cried. "Let's go see Lola right now!"

"Calm down, Janey," Lolli's father said with a laugh. "These ladies need to get Red settled back in his stall first."

"Actually, maybe we don't." Mrs. Jamison glanced at Darby. "I wanted to try him out cross-country anyway. Feel like taking a hack?"

"A what?" Janey asked.

"She said a hack." Zach pretended to have a coughing fit.

Darby laughed. "Not that kind of hack," she said. "Hacking is just a horsey word for riding out." She nodded at Mrs. Jamison. "Let me grab a horse and my helmet and we'll go right now."

She hurried into the barn and returned moments later leading a stout brown horse.

"Can you give me a leg up?" she asked Ms. Tanaka.

"Aren't you forgetting something?" Zach asked. "Where's your saddle?"

Ms. Tanaka grinned. "Oh, Darby doesn't need a saddle," she told the kids. "She always did love riding bareback!"

She helped Darby vault onto the horse's back. Then she told her how to get to Lolli's farm.

"Great," Darby said. "We'll meet you there."

——————

"What if they got lost?" Lolli wondered, feeling her stomach flip over with worry. They were so close to finding Lola the perfect home—Lolli didn't want anything to ruin it now!

The Pet Rescue Club, Lolli's father, and Ms. Tanaka were back at Lolli's farm waiting for Darby and Mrs. Jamison to arrive.

"I'm sure they're not lost," Ms. Tanaka said. "Cars are faster than horses, you know."

Zach grinned. "Even racehorses?"

"Even racehorses," Ms. Tanaka replied. "I'm sure they—"

The rest of her words were lost in a loud whinny. Lola had been dozing by the fence while Lolli rubbed her neck. But now the pony raced along the fence, staring out across the driveway.

A second later, another whinny came from that direction. Then Red and Mrs.

Jamison came into view. Red was trotting toward the Pet Rescue Club with his ears pricked forward. Darby and her horse were right behind him.

"It looks like we found the right place," Mrs. Jamison called. "At least Red seems to recognize his friend!"

Lola started running back and forth on her side of the fence, whinnying and snorting. Janey had never seen her move so fast!

"Look—Lola thinks she's a racehorse, too," Zach joked.

Lolli couldn't respond. She was too busy watching as Red reached the pen. Mrs. Jamison let the reins go loose, and Red stretched his long neck over the fence, nuzzling at Lola. She stretched up, nuzzling him back.

"Well," Mrs. Jamison said with a smile. "I suppose this settles it. Lola will just have to come home with me and Red."

"Really?" Janey gasped. "That's awesome!"

"Yes, it is." Darby was smiling, too. "And to celebrate the happy occasion, I'll throw in some free training for Lola. I'm sure we can turn her into the perfect little riding pony for Mrs. Jamison's kids."

"Hooray!" Zach cheered.

"The Pet Rescue Club did it again," Janey exclaimed.

Adam grinned at Ms. Tanaka and Darby. "With a little help from our friends," he added. "Thanks, Ms. Tanaka!"

"I'm happy to help." The teacher winked. "After all, I owe you one. Without the Pet Rescue Club, I wouldn't have my Truman!"

Just then there was a flurry of excited barking from the direction of the house. Lolli's mother appeared, with Truman and Roscoe pulling at their leashes.

Meanwhile, Janey was still watching the happy reunion between Red and Lola. "We'll miss you, Lola," she said.

"Yeah," Lolli added. "But I won't miss

getting up at the crack of dawn to feed you."

Zach grinned. "And I won't miss flinging horse poo around."

"If you do, you can always come by my barn to help clean stalls," Mrs. Jamison told him with a chuckle. She glanced around at all the kids. "And I hope you'll all come by to visit Lola."

"Definitely," Janey promised.

Lolli's father smiled. "All's well that ends well," he said. "But maybe the Pet Rescue Club should stick to dogs and cats from now on."

Zach grinned. "We can't make any promises," he joked.

"May I borrow your phone?" Lolli asked her mother. "I want to call the shelter and let Kitty know we found a perfect home for Lola."

"Of course." Mrs. Simpson fished her cell phone out of her pocket and handed it over.

Soon Lolli was talking to the shelter worker. Kitty was thrilled by the news about Lola. "Congratulations," she said. "But Lolli, I was just going to call you."

"You were? Was it about Lola?" Lolli asked.

"No, it's about the rabbit you saw the other day," Kitty said. "Someone wants to adopt him. It's a lady who has kept house rabbits all her life and saw our bunny's listing online. But since you said you might want to adopt the little guy, I thought I should check in first and see if you're still interested."

Lolli hesitated, remembering how soft and sweet the bunny was. Then she shook her head.

"Thanks for asking," she said. "But actually, taking care of Lola made me realize I might not be the best home for a rabbit after all. And that lady sounds perfect."

"I see." Kitty sounded impressed. "All right, then. The lady will be very happy!"

Lolli hung up and turned around to see Janey staring at her. "Was that about the bunny?" Janey sounded disappointed. "Are you sure you don't want to adopt him?"

Lolli stepped over to pet Roscoe. "I don't really need another pet right now," she said. She glanced at Lola and Red. "Not when there are so many animals out there who need my time and energy to find them homes."

"True." Janey smiled at her. "They definitely need you—and the rest of the Pet Rescue Club!"

Pony Prep

Are you ready for a horse or pony of your own? Or would a different kind of pet suit your lifestyle better? Take this quiz and find out!

Where do you live?

A) On a farm

B) In a suburban house with a yard

C) In a city apartment or condo

How much time can you spend with your new pet?

A) Lots of time—my pet is my hobby!

B) An hour or so per day

C) Only a little bit—I'm super busy!

How would you describe yourself?

A) I'm not afraid of hard work and getting dirty.

B) I love to play games and run around outside.

C) I like to relax, be comfortable, and keep my hands clean.

How much experience have you had with horses or ponies?

A) Tons of hands-on experience—I've taken riding lessons and/or worked on a horse farm.

B) Some experience—I've been on a trail ride, read lots of books about horses, and/or watched plenty of movies or videos about them.

C) Nothing—I don't know which end of the horse whinnies!

Results

Mostly As: If your answers were all or mostly *A*, congratulations! You just might be ready for pony ownership!

....

Mostly Bs: If your answers were all or mostly *B*, you might not be quite ready for a pony yet. Going on trail rides and reading books are good ways to learn, but you'll want to get more experience before you take the pony plunge. Ask your parents if you can take riding lessons to learn even more. In the meantime, your lifestyle might be better suited for a lively dog, puppy, or kitten!

Mostly Cs: If your answers were all or mostly *C*, you probably don't even want a pony. They require lots of knowledge and work—and some of that work can get you pretty dirty! You might get along better with a quiet adult cat, a tank of fish, or another smaller, less active pet.

....

Luckily, there are pets out there for all kinds of people! Check out the ASPCA website (www.aspca.org) for more tips on caring for horses and pets of all types.

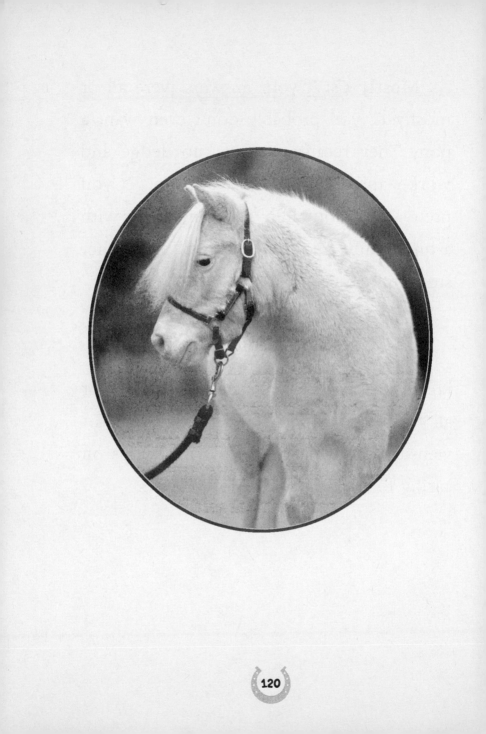

The Real Lola

Lola the homeless pony was inspired by a real-life animal rescue story. A famous show-jumping rider was at a big show, where she happened to meet a miniature horse (another kind of small equine) named Lola. When she found out that Lola had been headed to slaughter—and that she had a young foal—the rider decided to adopt them both! The real-life Lola and her son, Harley, now live happily on the rider's farm, where Harley is learning to be a tiny riding horse for the rider's young son.

Look for the next book in the **PET RESCUE CLUB** series!

**Book #4—
Too Big to Run**

Zach's mom has a new patient—a giant dog named Millie who has been helping her owner train for a marathon. Millie's knees can't handle all that running and now she needs an operation. Time for the kids in the Pet Rescue Club to help! Together they find a way to raise money for Millie's surgery and come up with a great way for Millie to find the perfect new career!